For my raging ramen monster—my son, Isaac
—P. T.

To my Hokkaido obaachan and my mom. You taught me about the deliciousness of ramen and the joy of cooking.
ラーメンの美味しさと料理の楽しさを教えてくれた北海道おばあちゃんと母へ。
—S. P.

ATHENEUM BOOKS FOR YOUNG READERS · An imprint of Simon & Schuster Children's Publishing Division · 1230 Avenue of the Americas, New York, New York 10020 · Text © 2023 by Patricia Tanumihardja · Illustration © 2023 by Shiho Pate · Book design by Karyn Lee © 2023 by Simon & Schuster, Inc. · All rights reserved, including the right of reproduction in whole or in part in any form. · ATHENEUM BOOKS FOR YOUNG READERS is a registered trademark of Simon & Schuster, Inc. Atheneum logo is a trademark of Simon & Schuster, Inc. · For information about special discounts for bulk purchases, please contact Simon & Schuster Special Sales at 1-866-506-1949 or business@simonandschuster.com. · The Simon & Schuster Speakers Bureau can bring authors to your live event. For more information or to book an event, contact the Simon & Schuster Speakers Bureau at 1-866-248-3049 or visit our website at www.simonspeakers.com. · The text for this book was set in Halewyn. · The illustrations for this book were rendered in sumi ink, pencil, and digital media. · Manufactured in China · 1122 SCP · First Edition · 10 9 8 7 6 5 4 3 2 1 · Library of Congress Cataloging-in-Publication Data · Names: Tanumihardja, Patricia, author. | Pate, Shiho, illustrator. · Title: Ramen for everyone / written by Patricia Tanumihardja ; illustrated by Shiho Pate. · Description: First edition. | New York : Atheneum Books for Young Readers, [2023] | Includes recipe. | Audience: Ages 4 to 8. | Audience: Grades K-1. | Summary: "A young boy aspires to make a bowl of ramen as delicious as his dad's, and runs into some surprises—both delightful and disastrous—on his first attempt"—Provided by publisher. · Identifiers: LCCN 2021035951 (print) | LCCN 2021035952 (ebook) | ISBN 9781665904353 (hardcover) | ISBN 9781665904360 (ebook) · Subjects: CYAC: Ramen—Fiction. | Food habits—Fiction. | Individual differences—Fiction. | Fathers and sons—Fiction. | LCGFT: Picture books. · Classification: LCC PZ7.1.T3815 Ram 2023 (print) | LCC PZ7.1.T3815 (ebook) | DDC [E]—dc23 · LC record available at https://lccn.loc.gov/2021035951 · LC ebook record available at https://lccn.loc.gov/2021035952

RAMEN FOR EVERYONE

Written by Patricia Tanumihardja

Illustrated by Shiho Pate

Atheneum Books for Young Readers
New York   London   Toronto   Sydney   New Delhi

こんぶ

にたまご

with nitamago egg,
the yolk golden like the sun;

Hiro loves ramen—
with nori seaweed,
briny like the ocean;

チャーシュー

with chashu pork
so tender, it melts in your mouth.

RAMEN 中

Most of all, Hiro wants to make the perfect bowl of ramen . . .

just like his dad,
   and his *dad's* dad before that.

Every Sunday, Hiro's dad makes ramen for dinner.

"When I was growing up in Hawai'i,
I watched Grandpa make ramen too," says Dad.
"That's how I learned."

First, Dad **Chops**, きる

Simmers, にこむ

and **seasons**.
あじつけ する

Grandpa's secret to a rich and flavorful broth . . .

. . . is patience!

Finally, Dad **shreds,**
きりさく

steeps,
つける

"And to finish, a choice of toppings for everyone . . ."

". . . because you can't argue with taste!" says Hiro.

Hiro has been studying Dad's technique for some time.
When his seventh birthday comes, Hiro decides he's ready.

"I'm a big boy now. I'm going to make the perfect bowl of ramen!"

The next day, Hiro studies his notes.

Dad's ramen noodles like your *eartobe* touch and try!

HOT be careful boiling water!

cut the noodles straight down

Dust with flour.

He puts on his apron.

He rolls up his sleeves.

Noodles, soft and springy.

But the seaweed crumbles.

The eggs slip through his fingers.

The pork falls apart . . .

. . . and there are no toppings for anyone.

The broth is bland.

The noodles are soggy.

And now the toppings
are unfit to eat.

Dinner is ruined!

Hiro rips off his apron . . .

. . . and throws everything into the trash.

"My ramen is horrible. It isn't perfect like yours."

"Ramen doesn't have to be perfect," says Dad.
"Mom and Mia are happy you're making dinner for them—
and I bet you can still make their ramen special."

That's it—Hiro has an idea!
Maybe he can save dinner after all.
Hiro tells Dad his plan, and they get to work.

"And some superspecial toppings coming right up!" says Hiro.

CHEESE

Hiro brings out big bowls of piping hot ramen.

"Dad, I know how much you like Hawaiian pizza. . . ."

THIS BOWL IS PERFECT FOR ME!

Hiro can't make broth that is rich and flavorful

YET!

or noodles that are soft and springy.

But he knows how to make perfect bowls of ramen for

Mom, Mia, Sushi

おかあさん　　みあねえちゃん　　すし

and Dad.

おとうさん

About Ramen

Ramen is a popular Japanese noodle dish believed to be of Chinese origin. Wheat noodles are served in a meat- or fish-based broth that is flavored with salt, soy sauce, and/or miso (a paste made with fermented soybeans, and rice and/or barley). Toppings such as egg, pork, sea vegetables, kamaboko (fish cake), and green onions finish off the dish.

Japanese people have been eating ramen for more than a century, but until recently, only prepackaged instant ramen (brands like Nissin and Maruchan) have been popular in the United States. Over the past decade, ramen shops taking after the traditional Japanese style have popped up across the country and can now be found in almost every major city. Modern American ramen chefs who are not as tied to tradition are becoming very creative with their ramen bowls, incorporating flavors like chili eggplant, curry chicken, and yes, even cheese or pineapple!

Ramen, like many other Asian noodle dishes, is all about personal preference. The rich, thick broth served at ramen shops is the result of simmering meat, bones, and/or vegetables for hours. However, many people make an easier version of ramen broth at home. When you make your own broth, you can add the condiments and spices you like best, including fiery hot sauce, sweet hoisin sauce, kimchi, vinegar, chili powder, and more! And when it comes to toppings, as Hiro has shown us, the sky is the limit! What will you put on *your* ramen?

Kitchen Rules

Cooking is a lot of fun, and by following a few simple rules, you can stay safe in the kitchen:

- Wash your hands with soap and water before handling food.
- Always have an adult assistant by your side to keep you safe, especially when using the stove or oven.
- Respect the knife. Practice with a plastic knife before upgrading to a real blade. Point the knife away from yourself and keep your fingers away from the blade while cutting.
- Mop up spills immediately to prevent slips and falls.
- Use pot holders or oven mitts when handling hot things.
- Turn pot and pan handles toward the back of the stove so they can't be accidentally knocked over.
- Taste, smell, listen, and look. Your senses will guide you in the kitchen.
- Relax and don't rush. Great cooking takes time!
- Have fun and cook for others—it will make them, and you, happy!

Easy Miso Ramen

For this recipe, you don't have to master noodle-making like Hiro; you can buy ramen or Chinese egg noodles at the grocery store. Plus, the broth is fast and simple to make using store-bought stock and miso paste.

Prep Time: 10 minutes (does not include making toppings)

Cook Time: 15 minutes

Makes: 4 servings

Ingredients

2 tablespoons sesame oil

3 cloves (1 tablespoon) garlic, peeled and minced

1-1/2 teaspoons fresh ginger, peeled and grated

1/4 cup chopped shallots

10 cups low-sodium chicken or vegetable stock

1/3 cup white miso

2 tablespoons sugar

2 tablespoons soy sauce (preferably Japanese shoyu)

2 teaspoons fine sea salt

1/2 teaspoon ground white or black pepper

8 to 10 ounces dried ramen or thin
   Chinese egg noodles

2 tablespoons mirin or dry sherry, optional

Suggested Toppings

Chashu or barbecued pork, store-bought or homemade

Pickled cucumbers or radishes

Hard-boiled eggs, halved

Buttered corn kernels

Toasted nori (seaweed)

Cooked vegetables like carrots, spinach, and bean sprouts

Chopped green onions (scallions) and extra sesame oil,
   for serving

Directions

1. **To make the broth,** heat the two tablespoons of sesame oil in a large pot over medium heat until shimmering hot. Fry the garlic, ginger, and shallots for about thirty seconds. (They should be browning a little and smelling great!) Pour in the stock, cover with a lid, and bring to a boil.

2. **While waiting for the stock to boil,** stir together the miso, sugar, and mirin or dry sherry (if using) in a small bowl. When the stock boils, adjust the heat until the broth is simmering (bubbling gently). Carefully ladle about half a cup of stock into the bowl and whisk. Pour the miso-stock mixture into the pot, followed by the soy sauce, salt, and pepper, and stir. Taste and adjust seasonings as needed. Keep the broth simmering while you cook the noodles.

3. **To cook the noodles,** bring a large pot of unsalted water to a boil. Add the noodles and cook according to the package instructions, stirring to loosen and unravel them. Hiro likes to cook his noodles until al dente (firm to the bite), about thirty to fifteen seconds earlier than the suggested time.

4. **To serve,** drain the noodles and then divide them among four large bowls. Pour 1 to 1-1/2 cups broth into the bowls and add your choice of toppings. Serve with green onions and sesame oil in little dishes on the side for people to add to their ramen if they wish.

いただきます!
I ta da ki ma su!